The Magic Hat

by Miriam Sklar

ISBN: 978-1-338-75083-6
Illustrated by John Lund

Published by Scholastic Inc., 557 Broadway, New York, NY 10012

10 9 8 7 6 5 4 68 25 26 27/0

Printed in Jiaxing, China. First printing, January 2021.

A rabbit is in the hat.

A skate is in the hat.

An eight is in the hat.

A clown is in the hat.

A crown is in the hat.

A mouse is in the hat.

A house is in the hat!